DUMB AND DUMBER

A novelization by Madeline Dorr
Based on the screenplay by Peter Farrelly,
Bennet Yellin, and Bob Farrelly

A PARACHUTE PRESS BOOK

Troll Associates

Copyright © 1994 New Line Productions, Inc. All rights reserved.
All photography © 1994 New Line Productions, Inc. All rights reserved.
Photo credits
Mark Fellman: p.49, p.50, p.51, p.52, p.53, p.54, p.55, p.56 (top).
B. Little: p.56 (bottom).
Cover photo by B. Little.
With special thanks to Fran Lebowitz, Judith Verno, and Susan Kaplan.

Printed in the U.S.A.
December 1994
ISBN: 0-8167-3695-2
10 9 8 7 6 5 4 3 2 1

CHAPTER ONE

It was as pretty as a day could be in Providence, Rhode Island.

A lovely young woman stood on the street corner, holding a heavy armload of books and squinting up at the cloudy March sky. A black stretch limousine glided past her, then squealed to a stop and backed up quickly.

After a moment, one of the darkened rear windows zipped down, revealing Lloyd Christmas. He was about 30 years old and had a pleasantly goofy smile and straight hair.

"Excuse me," he said, straightening the crooked knot in his tie. "Can you tell me how to get to the medical school? I'm supposed to be giving a lecture in 20 minutes, and my driver's a bit lost."

"Go straight aheads and makes a left over ze bridge," the young woman said with a heavy European accent.

"You from Jersey?" Lloyd asked cheerfully.

The young woman looked at him and scowled. "Austria."

"Austria?" Lloyd repeated. He put on a mock *Australian* accent. "Well, g'day, mate. What do you say we get together later and throw a few shrimp on the barbie?"

The young woman rolled her eyes and walked away.

Lloyd sighed and pushed a button, closing the window again. He sat for a minute, defeated. Then he climbed through the driver's partition and dropped into the front seat. He sighed again and put on a chauffeur's hat.

Lloyd wasn't the limousine's passenger—he was the driver!

Nearby, Harry Dunne sped out of a fast-food restaurant. He was dressed in a ridiculous beagle costume, complete with floppy ears. He walked over to a parked van. The van looked like a giant dog. It had four legs hanging off the sides, a tail in the rear, and, instead of a front grille, a dog's muzzle. The company name, Mutt Cutts, was painted along the side.

Whistling happily, Harry got into the van and opened his fast-food bag. "Okay, the double-decker's mine," he said. "Who had the Wiener schnitzel?"

A perfectly groomed poodle stuck his head into the driver's seat from the back of the van.

"Here you go, Dolph." Harry handed him his

food. "And the roast beef sandwich *au jus?*"

A delicate French poodle, coiffed to the max with ribbons and pom-poms, came forward.

"*Bon appétit*, Sweet'n Low," Harry said. "All right, who's got the foot-long?"

A toy poodle yapped.

"Very funny, Rascal," Harry said. He gave the wienie to a much larger poodle.

Just then a voice boomed over his CB radio.

"Harry," it screamed, annoyed. "Why haven't you dropped those dogs off at the show yet?" It was his boss, Mr. Palmer—and he was not happy.

"I wasn't about to send them to a performance on an empty stomach, sir," Harry said.

"Well, Mrs. Neugeboren called. She's been waiting for two hours," Palmer answered. "Get a move on it!"

"You got it," Harry said. He snapped to attention. Then he put on his Walkman, started whistling, and slammed the accelerator to the floor.

The van kicked into high gear, sending the dogs bouncing around in the back. Harry drove wildly down a hill and skidded around a corner. The dogs slid left, then right, and then backward. A woman pushing a baby carriage crossed the street. Harry narrowly missed hitting her. Then he took another corner on two wheels. Finally he screeched to a halt in front of the dog-show auditorium. From behind, there was a loud thump as the poodles bounced off their seats again.

Harry hopped out of the van and opened the back door. "Okay, gang, you know the rules," he said. "No pushing, no shoving. Please exit in an orderly fashion."

An angry Mrs. Neugeboren teetered down the sidewalk on high heels. "Where have you been?" she yelled. "Now I hardly have any time to primp the dogs!"

"Don't worry," Harry said proudly. "These pooches don't *need* any primping. I stand by my work."

Mrs. Neugeboren took one look inside the van and screamed.

Harry turned. The beautifully groomed dogs now looked like frazzled, shivering strays. Their fur was covered with ketchup and mustard.

"You, uh, might just want to run a comb through them," he said. He ducked before Mrs. Neugeboren could hit him with her umbrella.

Lloyd pulled his limousine into a long, tree-lined driveway. He got out, gazing in awe at the impressive stone mansion. He smoothed his hair slightly before walking up to the front door to ring the bell.

The double doors opened, and the most gorgeous woman he could imagine appeared. She looked about 25 years old with shining hair and trusting eyes.

Lloyd's jaw dropped. "Oh, my," he whispered.

"Hello," she said softly. "I'll just be a minute."

As she stepped back inside, Lloyd whipped out a tiny can of breath spray. He aimed the spray at his mouth—and missed completely. Unseeing, he went to put the can away. It clattered to the ground without him noticing.

The woman came out again. Lloyd held the car door open for her. Then he sped around to the driver's seat. The woman sat quietly, clutching a leather briefcase on her lap.

Lloyd peered in the rearview mirror as he drove, trying to think of something charming to say.

"Why are you going to the airport?" he asked. "Flying somewhere?"

"How'd you guess?" she answered dryly.

"Well..." Lloyd thought about that. "I saw your luggage, and then when I noticed the airline ticket, I put two and two together. Plus, it's written on the order." He paused. "So, where you heading?"

"Aspen," she said, staring out the window.

Lloyd nodded several times. "Yup, California's beautiful this time of year." He cleared his throat. "Name's Christmas. Lloyd Christmas."

"I'm Mary Swanson," she said without much interest.

Lloyd nodded again, trying to think of another way to impress her. "Uh, this isn't my real job, you know. It's only temporary." He checked his rearview mirror to see if she was listening. "You see, my friend Harry and me are saving up our money so we can open our own pet store."

"That's nice," Mary said vaguely.

Lloyd gave her a toothy smile. "I got worms," he announced.

Mary looked startled. "I beg your pardon?"

"That's what we're going to call it," Lloyd explained. "I Got Worms. We're gonna specialize in selling worm farms. You know, like ant farms. A lot of people don't realize that worms make much better pets. They're quiet, they don't bite, and they're super with the kids."

"Aren't *ants* quiet too?" Mary asked.

"Yeah," Lloyd admitted. "But if you cut their heads off, they won't grow back."

Mary frowned.

"Best of all, worm farming is a *$75,000-a-year* industry." Lloyd chuckled. "I wouldn't mind having a chunk of *that* pie, if you know what I mean."

To her credit, Mary had no idea what he meant.

"What's the matter?" Lloyd asked in concern. He could see that her mind was elsewhere. "Little tense about the flight?"

Mary hesitated. "Something like that," she replied.

Lloyd swiveled around to look at her. The steering wheel spun, and the limousine aimed at an oncoming car. "It's really nothing to worry about. Statistically, they say you're more likely to get killed *on the way* to the airport." They narrowly missed the other car. "Like in a head-on crash."

As he kept talking, he ran a red light. "Or getting trapped under a gas truck. That's the worst. I have this cousin—" He stopped. "Well, *had* this cousin, and one time, he—" A second oncoming car blared its horn in warning.

"Um, Lloyd, could you please keep your eyes on the road?"

Mary's eyes widened with each near-miss.

"Good thinking," Lloyd said. Cheerfully, he turned to face the road again. "Can't be too careful, there's a lot of bad drivers out there."

Once they got to the airport, Lloyd loaded Mary's bags onto a cart and slammed the trunk. She reached into her purse and pulled out a ten-dollar bill.

"Here you go." Mary looked around nervously.

"No, no, I couldn't possibly accept this," Lloyd said in a hearty voice. "Not after what we've been through."

Mary managed a weak smile. "Well, thanks, Lloyd," she said. "And good luck with your worms."

Lloyd held his arms out wide, and reluctantly, Mary moved into his embrace.

"Oh, I hate good-byes." Lloyd sighed, holding her close.

Mary tried to pull free. "Uh, Lloyd—"

He let her go, and then he put his index finger to her lips. "Shhh," he whispered. "Just go."

She frowned, picking up her briefcase and luggage. Lloyd watched her head for the terminal. He sighed again, enchanted and lovesick.

The most perfect woman in the world for him had just walked right out of his life.

◀ CHAPTER TWO ▶

Mary plowed through the throng of travelers. Her eyes were narrowed and her shoulders were tense. She passed a row of phone booths, and two suspicious-looking thugs—a woman in an expensive tailored suit and a man in a plaid sport coat—spied her.

"She's going to leave the briefcase at the foot of the escalator," the man in the plaid sport coat said. "You make the pickup."

"Piece of cake," the woman in the tailored suit answered.

Outside, Lloyd had just started the limo. As it slid forward, he spotted Mary walking inside the airport. He beeped the horn and waved, trying to get her attention. The limo bumped into the parked car in front of him. Instantly, the limousine's protective airbag inflated.

Mary glanced outside and saw that the airbag had squished Lloyd's face. He smiled sheepishly and waved. Mary waved back without enthusiasm and put down her briefcase. She checked her coat pockets for her ticket. Then, still searching, she started up the escalator with her luggage. The briefcase was left behind.

"There, she left it." The man in the plaid coat nudged his partner. "Let's go."

But Loyd saw that Mary had forgotten her briefcase. He squeezed out from behind the airbag and leapt out of the limousine. He raced into the terminal, grabbing the handle of the briefcase just as the female thug started to reach for it.

"Coming through!" Lloyd shouted. He tore up the escalator three steps at a time.

Below him, the thugs stared at each other, dumbstruck.

Briefcase in hand, Lloyd dashed to the TV monitors that posted the departure times. He scanned the flight numbers, then darted away. In his way stood a nurse holding a charity bucket. He knocked her aside.

"Move it or lose it, sister!" He ran frantically through the airport.

Finally, he reached the gate marked Aspen and sped into the jetway. An airline attendant tried to stop him.

"Sir, you can't go in there," she said.

"It's okay!" Lloyd yelled, pointing to his name tag. "I'm a limo driver!"

A moment later a scream of pain and frustration rang out. Lloyd lay sprawled on his back on the ground, 20 feet below the airport gate. From the entrance to the jetway the flight attendant stared at him in disbelief. The plane had already pulled away. Lloyd had been running too fast to stop and had dashed into thin air.

After moaning for a while, Lloyd pulled himself to his feet and limped back into the terminal. He passed the two thugs, who followed him at a safe distance. He managed to drag himself outside, then he stopped dead in his tracks. His limo was being towed away.

"Great," he said. He tossed his chauffeur's cap into the trash. "Just great."

Much later Harry parked his Mutt Cutts van in front of his apartment building. At the same time, a taxi pulled up and let Lloyd out.

"How was your day?" Harry stretched and stared at his buddy.

Lloyd sighed heavily. "I've had worse. How about yourself?"

"Oh, you know." Harry slogged up the front steps. "Same old, same old."

Across the street, a black Cadillac pulled up and parked. Inside sat the two thugs. The woman in the tailored suit, known to her partner as J. P. Shay, sat and scowled. Beside her, Joseph Mentalino—better known as Mental—reached into his pocket for a pillbox and poured a handful of pink antacid tablets into his mouth.

"Who do you figure this guy's working for?" Mental asked.

Shay shrugged and watched as Mental shook out more pills.

"Your ulcer?" she asked.

"It ain't gonna kill me," Mental said grimly, chewing away.

Upstairs, Lloyd and Harry dragged themselves into their apartment. They plunked down in their favorite easy chairs. Harry's parakeet, Petey, tweeted a lively hello, but the guys just sat there in silence.

The place was a mess. Shreds of wallpaper hung from the walls. The carpet was threadbare.

"So, you got fired again, huh?" Harry asked.

"Well, technically I quit," Lloyd replied.

"Why'd you do that?" Harry asked.

Lloyd shrugged. "I had a hunch Arnie was going to fire me anyway."

Harry nodded. "I lost my job too."

"Really?" Lloyd laughed. "Man, you are one pathetic loser. No offense."

"None taken," Harry said.

They sat there.

"The worst part is," Harry said, "I just spent my life savings turning my van into a poodle."

"Yeah, but you probably would've done that anyway," Lloyd pointed out.

Harry nodded and let out an enormous burp.

"What's with the briefcase?"

"It's a love memento," Lloyd said. "From the most beautiful woman alive. Mary. I drove her to the airport. Sparks flew, emotions ran high. She actually *talked* to me, man. Right *to* me. Then she left this case behind and flew out of my life."

"What's in it?" Harry asked.

"Harry, only a lowlife would go snooping around in other people's private property."

Harry paused. "Is it locked?" he asked.

Lloyd nodded. "Yeah, really well."

There was a loud knock on the door. Petey squawked in alarm.

"Friend or foe?" Lloyd called.

"We don't have any friends," Harry reminded him. He tiptoed to the peephole and looked out. Shay and Mental waited at the door. Mental was holding a gun. "There's two of them. And one's got a gun."

Lloyd thought about that. "Gas company?"

Harry shrugged. "Yeah, probably. I say we bail."

Lloyd grabbed the briefcase. He and Harry bolted to the window and scampered down the fire escape. They jumped into the Mutt Cutts van.

"Where should we go?" Lloyd asked.

Harry shrugged, then gunned the motor. "Unemployment, where else?"

The two thugs burst into the now-empty apartment. Shay and Mental wasted no time, searching everywhere, tossing the guys' few possessions to the floor.

"The briefcase ain't here," Mental announced. "He must've taken it with him."

"Well, he's gotta come home sometime," Shay said.

"Maybe we should leave him a little message." Mental approached the parakeet's cage. "Let them know we're playing hardball." He wrapped his meaty fist around the bird.

There was a screech of terror, and Petey fell over, dying of fright.

"He taut he taw a puddy tat." Mental held the bird close to his mouth and laughed an evil laugh.

An hour later Lloyd and Harry shuffled somberly out of the unemployment office.

"Our counselor had a bit of an attitude," Lloyd said.

"Yeah," Harry agreed. "He must still be mad about you getting fired from that snowplow job."

"Well, I missed only three days of work in two months." Lloyd looked hurt. "And that was because of a blizzard."

Harry nodded sympathetically.

Back at home, Lloyd put down the briefcase. "Give me what's left of our dough," he said to Harry. "I'll go buy a few necessities."

Harry handed him some crumpled bills. "Good plan."

Leaving the briefcase with Harry, Lloyd hurried to the store, where he bought some necessities—pinwheels, a bolo bat, marbles, jacks, and a king-size Styrofoam cowboy hat. Finished, he stopped outside at a newspaper machine. He pulled out his wallet and removed a quarter.

He dropped the quarter in, opened the machine, and realized that he didn't have a free hand. So he put his wallet inside the machine and picked up the newspaper. The door slammed shut—with his wallet locked inside.

Lloyd sighed and checked his pockets for more change. When he didn't find any, he stopped an elderly woman cruising slowly by on her motorized cart.

"Excuse me, little old lady," he said politely. "Do you have change for a dollar?"

"No, I'm sorry," she said. "I don't."

"Well, could you do me a favor and guard this while I go in the store to get some?" he asked. "My wallet's locked in the machine, and I need someone I can trust to stay here."

"Of course," the elderly lady said sweetly.

Lloyd gave her a grateful smile. "I guess they're right," he said. "Senior citizens, although slow and dangerous behind the wheel, can still serve a purpose."

Lloyd was gone for only a minute. When he came back outside, the newspaper-machine glass was broken. His groceries and wallet were nowhere in sight, and neither was the little old lady!

CHAPTER THREE

His life had become a disaster. Discouraged, Lloyd trudged home empty-handed. He found Harry sitting on the couch with his head in his hands. On his face was a look of despair.

"It's all gone," Lloyd said. "I got robbed by a little old lady." He shook his head in disgust. "And I didn't even see it coming."

Harry whimpered.

"Cheer up, man," Lloyd said. "We've been down and out before. We'll land on our heads somewhere."

"It gets worse," Harry said. "It's Petey, he's—dead."

Tears filled Lloyd's eyes. "Oh, man, I'm sorry. What happened?"

"His head fell off," Harry said, choking.

Lloyd stared at him. "His *head* fell off??"

"Yeah." Then Harry sighed. "He was pretty old."

It was all so unfair.

"That's it!" Lloyd shouted. "I've had it with this dump! We don't have food, we don't have jobs, our pets' heads are falling off—we've got to get out of this town, Harry!"

"And go where?" Harry asked miserably.

"Someplace warm," Lloyd said. "A place where beautiful women instinctively flock like the salmon of Capistrano." He paused dramatically. "I'm talking about a little place called Aspen."

Harry shook his head. "Aspen? I don't know, Lloyd, the French are jerks."

"Let me ask you something," Lloyd said. "Do you want to end up like poor old Petey, dead in some flea-ridden apartment with a soggy sunflower seed pressed to your beak? No! Don't you see what Petey was trying to say to you? You've got to grab life, chew it up, and spit it out. Spread your wings and run, run, run!"

Harry looked confused. "I don't know, Lloyd. I think his head just fell off." Then he got it. "Wait a second! You just want to go find that girl who lost her briefcase, and you need *me* to drive you there."

"Psychic hotline!" Lloyd said cheerfully.

"I don't know, Lloyd," Harry said, clearly torn. "I think we should stay here, hunt for jobs, and keep saving up for the worm store. Make something of ourselves."

Lloyd moved to the window and looked out at the wintry gray cityscape. "You know what I'm sick and tired of, Harry? I'm sick and tired of having to eke my way through life. I'm sick and tired of being a nobody. And most of all, I'm sick and tired of *having* nobody."

There was a short silence.

"Okay, Lloyd," Harry said. "Aspen it is."

They hugged, and then Harry approached Petey's cage, his eyes overflowing with tears.

"Petey, I made a promise to you once," he said. He thought hard. "I *really* wish I could remember what it was."

So Lloyd and Harry took to the open road in the Mutt Cutts van, ready for adventure.

"Well, we're finally doing it." Lloyd's eyes shone with excitement. "Do you realize we've never taken a trip together? This is *great!*"

Harry nodded, unbuckling his seat belt.

"Why'd you take off your seat belt?" Lloyd asked.

Harry shrugged. "Because we just cleared the danger zone. Don't you know anything? Ninety percent of all accidents happen within five miles of home. We've already traveled 6.3 miles."

Lloyd considered that. "Well, what about the people who live around here? What if we get into an accident with one of them?"

Harry sheepishly put his seat belt back on.

"That's right—got you." Then Lloyd ripped open a bag of Doritos to celebrate.

"Where'd you get those?" Harry asked. "We're on a tight budget, remember?"

"This didn't come out of our travel fund," Lloyd assured him. "I was able to scrape up 25 extra bucks before we left."

Harry glanced over doubtfully. "How?"

"I sold some stuff to some kid," Lloyd said, crunching his chips a handful at a time.

Harry frowned. "Exactly what did you sell?"

"Stuff," Lloyd said.

"Lloyd—what *kind* of stuff?" Harry asked.

Lloyd looked guiltily out the window. "Oh, a few baseball cards, a sack of marbles, Petey, three comic books—"

Harry stared at him. "Are you telling me you sold my dead bird?"

"Uh-huh," Lloyd mumbled.

"But—" Harry stopped. "Petey didn't have a head...."

"Don't worry," Lloyd said, looking annoyed. "I taped it back on."

"Oh," replied Harry, scratching his head.

Back at the apartment, Mental and Shay found a note on Lloyd and Harry's door.

It read: DEAR GAS MAN—PACKED UP AND DROVE TO ASPEN. SORRY ABOUT THE MONEY. LLOYD AND HARRY.

Mental scowled. "Those losers are rubbing it right in our faces."

Shay nodded. "Andre will have a fit if we don't

22

get that briefcase back soon."

Mental ripped the note off the door. "Gas man," he said and rubbed his stomach. "How did they know I've got gas?"

"They must be pros," Shay said. "We may never see that money again."

"Don't worry, we'll get it back," Mental promised. "And I'll tell you something else. They are *never* going to reach Aspen either. I'll make sure of that if it's the last thing I ever do!"

Several hours later, Lloyd and Harry had made it all the way to Pennsylvania.

"How far have we gone?" Harry asked.

Lloyd studied the map on his lap. "About an inch and a half."

"How much farther do we have to go?" Harry asked.

Lloyd traced their route with his finger. "About a foot."

Harry made a face. "We're going to need a smaller map, or we'll never get there. We don't have enough gas money."

"Relax," Lloyd said. "We have more than enough."

"I believe you're wrong, Lloyd," Harry said.

Lloyd wrinkled his forehead. "And I believe I'm *right*, Harry. How much you want to bet?"

"I don't bet," Harry said.

Lloyd looked at him incredulously. "What do

you mean you don't bet?"

"I don't gamble, you know that." Harry switched lanes without signaling. "Never have and never will."

"Yeah, sure," Lloyd said. "I bet I can get you gambling before the day is over."

Harry stuck out his hand. "How much?"

"Twenty bucks," Lloyd said.

"You're on!"

"I'm going to get you," Lloyd said smugly. "I don't know how, but I'm going to get you."

"Never happen," Harry promised.

A little while later they pulled up at a truck stop. They sat in a small booth surrounded by tough-looking truckers. Their middle-aged, no-nonsense waitress dumped two hamburgers and two sodas on the table.

"Uh, excuse me, Flo," Lloyd said, although he had no idea what her name was. "What's the soup *du jour?*"

"It's soup of the day," the waitress said grumpily. "And it isn't Flo."

Lloyd nodded. "That sounds good. I'll have that."

"Anything else?" she asked sarcastically.

"Yeah, my soda's flat," Harry said. "It doesn't have any bubbles."

The waitress picked up the glass and blew hard into the straw, bubbling the drink. "Happy now?" she snapped and stomped away.

"Feels good to mingle with these laid-back countryfolk, don't it, Harry?" Lloyd asked.

Harry didn't answer. He was too busy wiping his straw with a napkin. As he wiped, he accidentally knocked over the salt shaker.

"Uh-oh," Lloyd said. "Spilling salt is very bad luck. We're driving across the country—the last thing we need is bad luck. Quick, toss some over your right shoulder."

"What for?" Harry asked.

"Because that's *good* luck," Lloyd said.

Harry threw the salt shaker over his shoulder. Behind them there was a loud yelp. Lloyd glanced over to see a burly, surly trucker wiping salt out of his eyes.

"Too little too late, Harry," Lloyd remarked.

The huge trucker stood up, putting his hands on his hips. "Okay!" he shouted at the top of his lungs. "Who's the dead man?"

Everyone in the restaurant—including Lloyd—pointed at Harry.

"I-it was a terrible accident, sir," Harry stuttered. "Believe me, I would never do anything to offend a man of your size. Please accept my most sincere apology."

The trucker growled and swaggered over to Lloyd and Harry's table, egged on by his equally burly friends.

"Teach him a lesson, Sea Bass!" one of them yelled.

The huge trucker towered over Harry while Lloyd, eating his hamburger, studied the jukebox menu hung over their booth.

Sea Bass glared down at Harry's plate. "You gonna eat that?"

"The—um—thought crossed my mind, sir," Harry said.

Sea Bass leaned over and spat a big brown wad of chewing tobacco onto Harry's hamburger. "Still want it?" he asked.

Harry shook his head. Laughing, Sea Bass picked up the burger and walked back to his table.

Their waitress slapped the bill on the table. Harry picked it up and sighed.

"Perfect," he said. "I'm out eight bucks and I still haven't eaten."

Lloyd blotted his mouth with a napkin. "Well, if you'd stop picking fights with the locals...." Then he brightened. "Wait, I have an idea." He got up and walked over to Sea Bass and his pals. "Excuse me, gentlemen. I'd just like to apologize for that unpleasant scene a little earlier."

Sea Bass looked at him blankly. "Hunh?"

Lloyd smiled at him. "What I'm trying to say is, my friend Harry and I would like to buy you guys a round of drinks, just to bury the hatchet."

Harry stared at Lloyd as though he had lost his mind, but the truckers seemed to like the idea.

"Make it four boilermakers," Sea Bass said.

Lloyd grinned. "Whatever you want, sir. I'll have the waitress send them over immediately. Oh, and, fellas—hope to see you again down the road."

"Lloyd, what are you doing?" Frantically, Harry followed his friend to the cashier. "We can't afford that!"

Lloyd handed the cashier their check. "Excuse me," he said. "Sea Bass and the fellas offered to pick up our check. They said just add this to their tab." He smiled. "They're very nice."

The cashier looked skeptical. "*Sea Bass* said that?"

"Well, if that guy over there is Sea Bass." Lloyd pointed across the dining room as Sea Bass nodded to the cashier and gestured to his table, not wanting to miss out on the free drinks.

"Okey-dokey," the cashier said. "If that's what he wants."

Harry grinned, grabbing a couple of beef jerkies, a candy bar, and a *National Enquirer*. "Oh, and put these on too."

"You got it," the cashier said, ringing them up.

"By the way—" Lloyd pitched his voice extra loud. "How far is it to Rhode Island from here? Because that's where we're going, you know."

"Rhode Island!" Harry said, horrified. "But—"

Lloyd flashed Harry a secret wink and a toothy grin. "Let's go," he said loudly, grabbing Harry's arm and pulling him toward the door. "It's a very long drive to Providence."

They rushed outside to the Mutt Cutts van. They didn't notice that Mental and Shay stood near the gas pump, filling their black Cadillac. The two thugs smiled wickedly and then jumped into their car, ready to follow the van. Now they would make Harry and Lloyd pay for all the trouble they had caused.

Seconds later Sea Bass realized he had been tricked. He stormed out of the diner, followed by his red-faced buddies.

"They're dead!" he shouted. "I'm gonna tear them apart!"

CHAPTER FOUR

Harry and Lloyd drove happily onto the highway, completely unaware of how many people were after them.

"That was genius, Lloyd," Harry said. "Sheer genius. Where'd you come up with a scam like that?"

"Saw it in a movie," Lloyd said modestly.

"Incredible," Harry chuckled. "So, what happened? The guy tricks some sucker into picking up his tab, and he gets away with it scot-free?"

"No," Lloyd admitted. "Actually, in the movie they catch him about half a mile down the road and slit his throat from ear to ear." He paused. "It was really good."

Just then Harry and Lloyd felt a *boom!* The Mutt Cutts van was slammed from behind. They turned to see a big rig right on their tail. At the wheel was a furious Sea Bass.

"Wow," Lloyd said. "This is exactly like the movie."

"What do we do?" Harry yelled, panicking.

Lloyd took out some beef jerky. "Go faster."

Harry gulped and slammed the gas pedal to the floor. The Mutt Cutts van leapt forward with Sea Bass still following.

"It's working!" he said. "We're blowing his doors off."

Lloyd looked pained. "Harry, I know this isn't the best time, but—I have to go to the bathroom."

"This *isn't* the best time!" Harry shouted.

"Fine." Sulking, Lloyd gobbled down some more beef jerky.

Behind them, Sea Bass noticed his radar detector beeping, and he started to slow down. He really wanted to slaughter those two jerks without mercy—but the last thing he needed was a speeding ticket.

Harry glanced into his rearview mirror. "Hey, I think we're losing him!"

"Yahoo," Lloyd shouted.

Then, from out of nowhere, a state trooper on a motorcycle pulled up beside the van. "Pull over!" the cop yelled.

Harry checked the sweater he was wearing, then looked back at the trooper. "No, it's a *cardigan!*" he shouted back. "But thanks for noticing!"

Lloyd pushed over and hung out the driver's side window. "Yeah, killer boots, man!" he commented.

The trooper turned on his siren. "Pull your vehicle to the side of the road!" he ordered.

Harry gulped, meekly put on his signal, and guided his car into the breakdown lane. As he did, Sea Bass drove by doing a cautious 55 miles per hour. He honked and waved, and Lloyd and Harry feebly waved back.

After accepting their speeding ticket and exchanging good-byes with the state trooper, it was Lloyd's turn to drive. Harry promptly fell asleep, and as the sun went down, Lloyd began to dream about his fabulous future in Aspen.

He pictured himself walking up the steps of a luxurious chalet, carrying Mary's briefcase. He knocked tentatively on the door, and Mary opened it. She looked at the briefcase, and broke into the biggest, sweetest smile he had ever seen. Tears of joy slid down her cheeks. Lloyd and Mary embraced.

Next he imagined himself in a cozy ski lodge. A fire crackled in the background. He was telling jokes and stories, captivating Mary—and a crowd of ski-sweatered companions. Suddenly Lloyd pointed at a man's sweater. The man looked down, and before he knew what was happening, Lloyd had flicked him on the chin with his finger. What a great trick! The whole group doubled over in amusement. Her eyes bright with love and awe, Mary laughed and held Lloyd's other hand.

Meanwhile, miles of highway passed swiftly.

Now, in Lloyd's daydream, he and Mary were alone by the fire, staring deeply into each other's eyes. Setting aside his mug of hot chocolate, Lloyd leaned forward to kiss her. He moved closer, and closer—and saw a pair of headlights where her eyes used to be. The headlights flashed once and then again.

Lloyd blinked and shook his head. He was totally blinded. Then he suddenly realized that he was steering the Mutt Cutts van into the path of an oncoming 18-wheeler! He grabbed the steering wheel with both hands. At the very last instant he veered back into his lane, avoiding tragedy by a whisker.

Harry woke up, yawning. "Want me to drive, man?" he asked.

"No," Lloyd said, still shaking. "I'm cool."

They ended up checking into a seedy roadside motel called the Second Honeymoon. There was a large heart-shaped Jacuzzi in their room, so they decided to take a nice, relaxing soak. Of course, it would have been more relaxing if the couple in the next room hadn't been having a *loud* argument.

"This sure is the life," Lloyd said. "A cold drink, a hot tub, and paper-thin walls." He sighed. "You know, there's only one thing that could make this moment any better."

Harry looked up from his *National Enquirer*. "What's that?"

"If you were a *girl*."

"And if I didn't have a headache." Harry put down his paper. He looked around at the tacky decor. "I don't know, Lloyd. These places bring back too many memories."

"*Pourquoi?*" Lloyd asked, using the French for "why." He blew soap bubbles.

Harry waved them aside. "Ah, it was a few years ago."

"What happened?" Lloyd wanted to know. "Some little filly break your heart?"

"Nah, it was a *girl*," Harry said. "Fraida Felcher. We visited a place like this—not this classy, but nice."

Lloyd frowned. "Felcher? You mean the girl from Cranston?"

Harry looked over. "You know her?"

Lloyd laughed. "Oh, yeah." Then he caught himself. "I mean, I remember you talking about her."

Harry's expression was dreamy. "We had an incredibly romantic time. Boy, I thought we'd be together forever." He let out his breath. "Then, about a week later, right out of the blue, she sends me one of those John Deere letters."

"That's cold, Harry," Lloyd said. "She give you any reason?"

"I called her up, and she gave me some rap about me not listening to her enough or something like that." Harry shrugged. "I wasn't really paying attention. The thing that really hurts is, I think she was seeing another guy. Never did find out who."

With a guilty look Lloyd sank slowly into the Jacuzzi until he was almost underwater. If he remained lucky, Harry would never find out the truth. He was the guy! Meanwhile, he could enjoy relaxing in the tub.

How could Harry know that outside the black Cadillac was parked only a few cars over from the Mutt Cutts van? Shay sat in the front seat, loading her gun, while Mental was at the pay phone nearby, calling their boss. Nicholas Andre was relaxing at his getaway house in Aspen.

"The boys are holed-up for the night," Mental reported.

"What are they up to?" Andre demanded. "Is it possible they're feds?"

"Unlikely," Mental answered. "From what I've seen."

Outside the phone booth, a man eager to use the telephone tapped on the glass. He motioned for Mental to hurry up.

"How long are you going to be?" the man inquired.

"Hold on a second, Mr. Andre." Mental put the phone down. He motioned the man closer, and when he was about a foot away, Mental punched his hand through the glass of the booth, knocking the man out. Then he picked up the receiver again. "Sorry, boss. You were saying?"

"Look, Mental, just find out what's going on," Andre ordered. "I want to know who these guys are. Get the money back, and then get rid of *them*!"

"No problem," Mental said. "Consider it done."

CHAPTER FIVE

Out in Aspen, Mary Swanson paced back and forth in her father's impressive, antique-filled living room. Karl, her father, and Helen, his much younger second wife, sat on the couch, watching her.

"It just doesn't make sense," Mary said, wringing her hands. "I left the money exactly where they told me to."

Helen shook her head. "We should have called the authorities the moment we knew Bobby had been kidnapped."

"Now, Helen," Karl said patiently. "We've been through this already."

Mary was close to tears. "I'd never forgive myself if something happened to Bobby."

"Helen, stop upsetting my daughter." Karl glared at his wife. "She's been through enough already."

"It's not her fault, Daddy," Mary said. "We're all a little on edge." Things had been tense since

Bobby had disappeared.

At that moment the living room door opened, and Nicholas Andre—the very same man who had hired Mental and Shay—walked in. His manner was solemn, and his eyes seemed full of concern.

"Has there been any word, Mr. Swanson?" he asked.

Karl shook his head. "Nothing yet, Nicholas."

"Perhaps I should call off the Preservation benefit this weekend," Andre suggested with insincere respect. "Reschedule it."

"No, Nicholas," Helen answered. "We shouldn't do anything out of the ordinary."

"She's right," Karl agreed. "We have to carry on as usual. Especially you, Mary."

"What am I supposed to do?" Mary asked. "Go about my life as if everything were fine?"

"That's *exactly* what you should do," Karl said. "Go out, go skiing, socialize. Don't you see, honey? We can't let on that anything is wrong. If the press, or the police, get wind of this, the kidnappers might panic. Who knows what they'd do to poor Bobby then?"

Mary gasped, covering her eyes with her hands.

Karl reached out to touch her arm. "Don't worry, sweetheart. I'll do everything they ask. Nothing's going to happen to Bobby, I promise you."

Mary didn't believe him, but she tried to smile

bravely. For Bobby's sake, she was not going to fall apart!

The next day, after leaving the motel, Harry and Lloyd waited in line at McDonald's drive-thru window.

"That's two cheeseburgers, two fries, and two medium Cokes," the employee at the pickup window said.

Harry handed him a ten-dollar bill and took back his change. "Thanks," he said. Then, before the employee could give them the bag of food, he absentmindedly drove off.

"Here's the way I see it, Harry," Lloyd said. "Once we give Mary the briefcase, she'll be so grateful, she'll plug us right into the party circuit. After that we'll do a little of the ski scene, mix with the elbow-rubbers, and then when we've got everyone right where we want them, we'll pitch the worm-store concept."

"That's brilliant!" Harry said. "But what if someone steals the idea?"

Lloyd thought about that. "Oh, yeah. That could definitely happen." He thought some more. "Maybe we'll just ski."

A couple of miles ahead of them, the black Cadillac had pulled over to the side of the road. Mental jumped out of the car and propped the hood open.

"Lie down on the front seat," he told Shay as he

loaded his gun. "After they pick me up, I want you to follow us."

Shay followed his orders.

Cruising along in the Mutt Cutts van, something dawned on Lloyd.

"Hey, wait a second," he said. "Hold everything. Aren't you forgetting something?"

Harry racked his brain, but couldn't think of anything.

"Back at Mickey D's?" Lloyd prompted him.

Harry thought and thought, and then gave up. "What?"

"My *change*," Lloyd said.

"Oh," Harry said sheepishly and reached into his pocket. "Right. Sorry."

On the side of the road they spotted a man standing by a black Cadillac, waving both arms. Harry slowed down.

"You guys going as far as Davenport?" Mental asked. "My car died, and I'm late for a business meeting."

Harry and Lloyd exchanged glances.

"We don't usually pick up hitchhikers, but I'm going to go with my instincts on this one," Lloyd said, and opened the door. "Saddle up, partner."

Much to his dismay, Joe Mental ended up sitting snugly between them on the front seat. Lloyd reached across Mental and tapped Harry's shoulder.

"You're it," he said.

Harry tapped him back. "Now you're it."

Lloyd tapped him immediately. "You're it. Quitsies."

Harry tapped him. "Anti-quitsies," he shot back. "You're it. Quitsies. No anti-quitsies. No startsies."

Lloyd shook his head. "You can't do that. Stamped it."

"Can too," Harry said. "Double-stamped it. No erasees."

"Cannot," Lloyd said. "*Triple*-stamped it. No erasees. Touched blue, make it true."

Mental moaned and grabbed his stomach. "Can't we listen to the radio or something, fellas?"

"Radio?" Lloyd said. "Who needs a radio? Ready, Harry?"

The boys snapped their fingers a few times and then broke into song. They sang loudly and quite off-key.

Mental listened for a few seconds, gritting his teeth. He reached for his gun, but Harry suddenly hit the brakes and skidded to a stop. Beside the road stood a group of migrant workers.

"Yeah, pick 'em up," Lloyd agreed, and opened the door.

Ten migrant workers piled into the van, including a crying baby, who sat on Mental's lap. Mental groaned, popping antacid pills as fast as he could while the migrant workers sang along with Harry and Lloyd. With a groan, Mental covered his ears.

Andre was not paying him enough money for this.

By the time they dropped off the migrant workers, it was time to eat again. Lloyd and Harry— and Mental—pulled up in front of Dante's Inferno Cafe. The sign out front advertised THE HOTTEST CHILI PEPPERS EAST OF THE MISSISSIPPI. This was the kind of challenge Lloyd and Harry liked best.

"Want a pepper, Mr. Mental?" Lloyd asked once they had been seated.

Mental shook his head, gulping an antacid.

"I'll do one if you will, Lloyd," Harry said.

"Okay." Lloyd pushed the jar toward him. "You go first."

Harry pushed the jar back. "No, you go first."

Mental spit the words through his teeth. "Why don't you both go *at the same time?*"

Simultaneously, Lloyd and Harry bit into the little red peppers.

"Hmm, that's not so bad," Lloyd said.

"Yeah," Harry agreed. "More tingly than hot."

Then their eyes lit up, and they both shrieked in pain and started gasping for breath.

"Have some water," Mental said, a smile curling across his lips. "It'll help."

Lloyd and Harry gulped down their water,

which made their mouths burn even more.

"Aw, shucks, that's right," Mental chuckled. "Water just makes it worse." He stood up. "Excuse me, guys. I've got to make a call."

Outside, he found a pay phone and dialed Andre's number for further instructions.

"What did you find out so far?" Andre asked.

"Nothing yet, but at lunch I'm gonna shake 'em down for information." Mental paused. "Then I'm gonna kill them for dessert."

"Whatever you do, don't let them get any closer," Andre warned. "I don't need them running around Aspen."

Mental pulled a black vial of poison pills out of his jacket. "Relax," he said and laughed cruelly. "They won't be going *anywhere*—not after *I* take care of them."

CHAPTER SIX

Inside the restaurant Harry and Lloyd were still huffing and puffing and perspiring. Their hamburgers had arrived, but they were in no shape to touch them.

"That really wasn't very polite of him, was it?" Harry said. "Maybe we should loosen the screws on his chair."

Lloyd gave him a reproachful frown. "You know what the Bible says, Harry."

"You mean, turn the other cheek?" Harry asked humbly.

"No. An eye for an eye," Lloyd said. "Hand me the jar. We must fulfill the Scriptures."

Harry grinned as they loaded Mental's burger with chili peppers, hiding them under the lettuce.

Mental returned and sat down. "So," he said and picked up his burger. "Why are you fellas headed to Aspen? Vacation?"

"Why don't you eat up, and we'll tell you," Lloyd said, trying not to laugh.

"Doesn't look like you packed much." Mental held his hamburger in midair. "All I saw was a couple of bags—and that briefcase."

Lloyd shrugged. "The briefcase isn't even ours. Some lady left it at the airport, and we're bringing it back to her." He snickered. "Hey! How's your burger?"

Mental stared at him, stunned by this news. "You mean, you don't even *know* her?"

Lloyd shook his head. "Not really. I was just her limo driver." He took a bite of his burger. "My, this is *tasty*."

Mental laughed and chomped into his hamburger too. Almost immediately his look of anticipation was replaced by a look of horror. He fell off his chair, holding his stomach and moaning out loud.

"My ulcer," he gasped. "Quick...pills...in my coat."

Lloyd dropped to his knees, pounding on Mental's chest—trying to do CPR. Harry searched quickly through Mental's pockets. He grabbed the black bottle not knowing it held poison pills. He shook out some pills and handed them to Mental, who gulped them down. His face had just started to relax, when he saw the black bottle in Harry's hand.

"You—you—" he gurgled, and then he keeled over.

Mental was dead.

After calling an ambulance, Harry and Lloyd got back in the van. Lloyd was behind the wheel as they started driving again.

"I can't believe it," Harry said, badly shaken.

Lloyd looked thoughtful. "Life is a fragile thing, Har. One minute you're chewing on a burger, the next you're dead meat."

"But he blamed *me*," Harry said. "You heard him. Those were his last words."

"Well—not if you count that gurgling sound," Lloyd said.

"Oh," Harry said, and brightened. "Right."

Back at Dante's Inferno Cafe, the police arrived, along with the medical examiner and an ambulance.

"He was poisoned." The medical examiner held up the container of pills. "We found these by the body."

Detective Dale, who was in charge of the investigation, frowned and wrote carefully. "Poison, huh?"

Another police officer came over. "The waitress says he was with a couple of younger guys," he said. "They're the ones who called the ambulance, then they hit the road. Someone else heard them say they were driving to France."

Detective Dale frowned harder. "*France?*"

The police officer shrugged. "We got a report

they were seen heading west on I-80 toward Colorado."

"Got a make on the vehicle?" Detective Dale asked.

"Yes, sir," the officer said. "They were driving an '84 poodle."

Detective Dale did a double take. "An '84 what?"

"Well, it might have been a wirehaired terrier," the officer said seriously. "They're very similar in appearance."

Detective Dale closed his eyes. "Someone get me an aspirin," he said. *"Fast."*

Shay stood in the phone booth near the cafe, watching all of the activity with wide eyes. Quickly, she dialed Andre to give him the news.

"You heard me," she said. "He's dead. They killed him!"

Andre wiped a nervous hand across his forehead. "All right, I want you back here," he said. "If they're coming this way, I'm going to need you. Hurry!"

After hanging up, Andre went downstairs to his basement. There was a small box in the middle of the room, about two feet by three feet. Tiny as the box was, a muffled human voice came from inside it.

Andre gave the box a kick. "How you doing today, Bobby?"

There was an indistinguishable mumble.

"What's that you're saying?" Andre asked. "Oh, you're going to kill me when you get out of there? Ooh, I'm scared. Hey, would you like to have a smoke?" He smiled, lit a cigarette, and bent to puff smoke into a very small air hole in the box.

Instantly, the box started bouncing up and down, and the whimpering increased. Andre smiled again.

He had Bobby *right* where he wanted him.

Later that night Lloyd slept, his feet out the window and his head on Harry's lap. Harry felt pretty tired himself, but he doggedly kept driving.

When they were only 25 miles from the Colorado state line, Harry stopped to get some gas. He opened the passenger door, and Lloyd tumbled out onto the asphalt, still sound asleep.

"Come on, wake up," Harry said. "You pay, I'll pump."

Lloyd walked sleepily over to the cashier's window, pulling some limp bills from his pocket.

As Harry yawned and pumped gas, a Jeep pulled up beside him. The door creaked open and a long-legged, athletic beauty stepped out. She was gorgeous. Seeing her, Harry made a feeble attempt to brush his hair into place. He searched his brain for a good opening line.

Finally, he cleared his throat, pointing at the

skis on her roof rack. "Skis, hunh?" he said.

"That's right," the woman replied.

"Great," Harry said, very jolly. "They yours?"

She nodded.

"Both of them?" he asked.

"Well—yeah," she said uneasily.

Harry looked impressed. *"Cool."*

In the meantime, Lloyd decided to go to the men's room. While he washed his hands, he glanced at some graffiti on the wall. It read: FOR A WILD TIME, MEET ME HERE, MARCH 25, 2:15 A.M. He frowned and glanced nervously at his watch.

It was March 25, and it was exactly 2:15 A.M.!

At the same time, the door started to open. He quickly hid inside one of the stalls. The sound of heavy footsteps approached, and he saw a pair of size-16 work boots beneath the door. The stall handle jiggled, and he heard a low growl. Then the ominous boots moved away. Lloyd let out a sigh of relief.

Suddenly the door was kicked in, and a towering figure stood before Lloyd.

It was Sea Bass!

Lloyd Christmas is a chauffeur. And today his new passenger, Mary Swanson, is about to change his life forever!

Lloyd's best friend, Harry Dunne, is a driver too. Except all his passengers are dogs!

Splat! Lloyd crashes onto a landing strip—all because of Mary's mysterious briefcase!

"We've got to get out of this town, Harry!" Lloyd shouts. So they take off for Aspen.

On the road, Lloyd, Harry, and hitchhiker Joe Mental taste the hottest chili peppers east of the Mississippi!

"Lloyd, you drove halfway across the country in the wrong direction!" Harry yells in disbelief.

Lloyd, Harry, and Mary's briefcase finally make it to Aspen, Colorado, on an old, beat-up minibike!

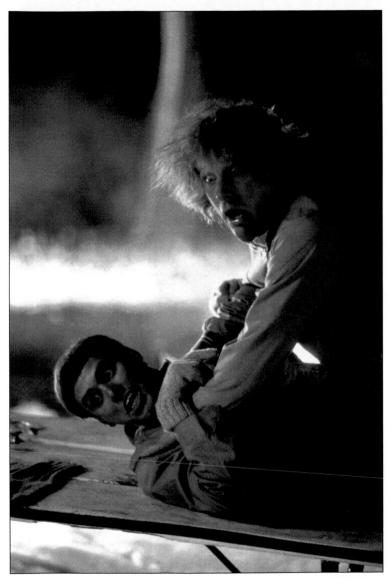

Lloyd and Harry fight moments before finding a fortune hidden in Mary's briefcase.

Lloyd is stunned to see Mary Swanson's picture in the local newspaper!

Mary Swanson is having a party. Lloyd and Harry get new haircuts for the big bash!

All dressed up and ready to celebrate!

Harry can't resist licking a patch of frost! And now he's stuck to it by the tip of his tongue!

Lloyd and Mary are handcuffed by thugs searching for the million-dollar briefcase.

Lloyd and Harry are ready for their next brainless adventure!

◄ CHAPTER SEVEN ►

Out by the gas pumps Harry was still trying to charm the beautiful woman, even though she had slid back into her car.

"That's, uh, a lot of luggage you have there," he commented.

"I'm moving to Aspen," she said. "My boyfriend's such a klutz, I've got to get away from him. My astrologer told me to avoid accident-prone guys."

Harry nodded in sympathy, leaning against her side-view mirror. The mirror snapped off the car, and Harry cracked his head against the windshield. Stunned, he fell down, then leapt to his feet as though nothing had happened.

"Here," he said, holding out the mirror. "This seems to be—loose."

She tossed it into the back seat, then took out a cigarette.

"Allow me." Trying to act smooth, Harry lit a match, then dropped it on the ground. He didn't notice that the match had set his left shoe on fire. "Look, uh, when I get to Aspen, maybe we can meet up—for hot chocolate, or something."

The athletic beauty smiled. "Why not? You seem pretty harmless. I'll give you my number."

As she rummaged through her purse, Harry smelled smoke. Glancing down, he saw that his left shoe was on fire! First he shook it. Then he tried to put out the fire with the other shoe. No luck!

"Look," he said urgently, jumping from foot to foot to try to put out the flames. "Why don't you just tell it to me? I've got a good memory."

She hesitated. "Are you sure you won't forget?"

"Positive!" Harry said, hopping around even more violently. "Please just hurry!"

"Okay," she said. "My number is 555-2553—oh, wait, that's my old number. It's so funny how your mind—"

"Just give me the stupid number!" Harry yelled.

She stared at him, taken aback by his outburst. "Well, if you're going to get pushy, just forget it!" She threw the car into drive and peeled away, leaving Harry in the dust.

Inside the men's room, Sea Bass wrapped his meaty paw around Lloyd's neck.

"What a nice coincidence," he growled. "First I'm gonna beat you to a pulp, and then I'm gonna kill you. Got any last requests?"

"Um, yeah," Lloyd said. "Could you do it the other way around?"

Just as Sea Bass drew his fist back, the men's-room door burst open and a flame-footed Harry rushed in. Panic-stricken, Harry plowed through the stall door—which hit Sea Bass on the head and knocked him out. Harry didn't even notice. He thrust his burning foot into the toilet, putting out the fire at last.

He let out a sigh of relief and looked around curiously. "Hey, whoa. Anything wrong, Lloyd?"

"Let's just get out of here," Lloyd said shakily.

They rushed back to the van and sped away. Later, when they were three miles from the Colorado state line, Harry yawned.

"Let's pull over and change seats," he said. "I've been driving for nine hours, and I'm too tired to start a new state."

They changed places. Harry settled gratefully into the passenger seat.

Lloyd cracked his knuckles. "Harry, you just sit back and enjoy the ride. You're in the hands of a *professional.*"

"Sounds good to me," Harry said, already half asleep.

At the state line the police set up a checkpoint, where they stopped and inspected cars. The police wanted to stop Harry and Lloyd before they could cross the border. A helicopter landed at the side of the road, and Detective Dale hopped out. He hurried to the cop in charge of the roadblock.

"Any sign of them yet?" he asked.

The cop shook his head. "No, but we're expecting them shortly. A motorist said he spotted a pooch about 30 miles out, headed this way."

Detective Dale smiled in satisfaction. He was certain they would catch the two friends. He settled back against the WELCOME TO COLORADO sign to wait.

Before he began driving, Lloyd decided to run into a nearby mini mart to stock up on snacks. By the time he got back, Harry was already fast asleep in the passenger seat.

Lloyd bit into a fresh package of beef jerky. "I love the open road," he said to no one in particular and then headed for the nearest freeway entrance.

As he entered the on-ramp, he passed a sign that said:

ROUTE 80—EAST. Without realizing it, he was headed right back home!

Harry slept through the night. He didn't move an inch—until the van hit a bump in the road. Then his eyes fluttered open, and he blinked at the bright sunshine. It was early in the morning.

"Hey, Mr. Sleepyhead," Lloyd said, sipping coffee. "Welcome back."

Harry rubbed his eyes. "How long have I been out?"

"I'd say a good five hours."

"Great." Harry stretched. "We must be getting real close, hunh?"

"Should be," Lloyd agreed. "I've been averaging about 90 miles an hour all night. Boy, this is one dangerous highway. You wouldn't believe all that road pizza—two dead coyotes, a couple of rabbits, and a huge deer."

"That's awful," Harry said. "Did you see the deer get hit?"

Lloyd shook his head. "No. I closed my eyes when it ran out in front of me, but I heard a big thud."

Harry gazed at the passing flatlands for several minutes. "Funny," he said. "I expected the Rocky Mountains to be a little rockier than this."

"I was thinking the same thing," Lloyd told him. "But that Des Moines is a pretty little town."

Harry started to nod, then realized what that meant. "Des Moines! Lloyd, refresh my memory: Doesn't the sun rise in the east and set in the west?"

"In our country it does, yes," Lloyd said kindly.

"Right," Harry said. "Then perchance you can explain to me why the sun is in our face at seven-thirty in the morning when we're heading *west*."

Lloyd thought about that—and then felt very, very sick.

Detective Dale and the other officers were still staked out at the Colorado border.

"It doesn't make sense," Detective Dale said impatiently. "They should've been here hours ago."

Another officer rushed over, holding his walkie-talkie. "We just got a report that they were spotted heading east near Des Moines on I-80."

Detective Dale looked incredulous. "Des Moines? But that's 500 miles from here!"

The other officers were stumped.

"Let's mobilize," Detective Dale said grimly. "Notify the other states too. Let's move!"

Back in Iowa, Lloyd and Harry stopped the van. Harry slumped onto the pavement beside it, his mouth still open in disbelief.

"I'm only human, Harry," Lloyd protested. "Anyone can make a little mistake. So we back-tracked a tad."

"A tad?" Harry shouted. "Lloyd, you drove halfway across the country *in the wrong direction!* Now we don't have enough money to get to Aspen, we don't have enough money to get home, we don't have enough to eat, we don't have enough to sleep!"

"It's not going to do any good to sit here and whine about it," Lloyd said huffily. "We're in a hole. We'll just have to dig ourselves out—"

"You know, you're absolutely right, Lloyd." Harry stood up. He brushed off his pants and started walking away.

"Where you going?" Lloyd asked.

"Home," Harry said sarcastically. "I'm walking home. We're probably only five miles away *anyway*."

"Oh, excuse me, Mr. Perfect," Lloyd called after him. "I guess I forgot that you never, ever make a mistake!"

Harry stopped short. "You've got a good reason to go. A beautiful girl's waiting for you. But let's face it, Lloyd, there's nothing waiting for me in Aspen. There nothing's waiting for me *anywhere*." He turned and headed for the open road.

Lloyd stood speechless, watching as his best friend deserted him in the middle of Iowa.

CHAPTER EIGHT

Harry walked slowly down the highway, his thumb stuck out. He was having no luck at all. A station wagon roared by, and a bag of garbage came flying out the window. It landed at his feet, and Harry stared at the litter, a tear slowly rolling down his cheek.

Then a high-pitched whirr sounded behind him.

"Hey, Harry!" he heard Lloyd shout. "Wait up!"

Harry turned and was stunned to see Lloyd riding a minibike.

"Got room for one more, hop on!" Lloyd said cheerfully.

Harry looked the minibike over. "Where'd you get it?"

"Some kid back in town," Lloyd said. "I traded the van for it." He smiled proudly. "This baby gets *70* miles to the gallon."

Harry shook his head. "You know, Lloyd, just

when I think you couldn't possibly be any dumb-
er, you do something great like this!"

"Still want to go to Aspen?" Lloyd asked as
excited as could be.

Harry grinned and hopped aboard. "More than
ever!"

"All right!" Lloyd cried, and they chugged
down the highway.

They made amazingly good time, and before
they knew it, they were approaching downtown
Aspen. Lloyd took off his helmet. His face was
purple and his eyebrows were nearly frozen.
When he climbed off the bike, Harry stayed on
his back.

"Harry?" Lloyd called out, confused. "Harry,
where are you?"

"Back here," Harry mumbled through numb
lips. "I'm stuck."

Lloyd laughed and started prying him off. "Got
a bit nippy going through the pass, eh, Har?"

Once they had thawed out, they strolled down
the main street. The store windows were
crammed with beautiful things, and the people
around them were incredibly chic. Aspen was a
town *filled* with the rich and famous. They had
never seen anything like it.

"Isn't this incredible," Lloyd said. "What more
could two single guys ask for?"

"How about some food?" Harry asked.

"I'm fine," Lloyd answered. "I swallowed a few

bugs when we were driving."

A gorgeous woman in a tight-fitting ski outfit and her handsome boyfriend walked by hand in hand. Harry and Lloyd stared.

"Wow," Harry said, impressed. "What a body!"

"Yeah," Lloyd agreed. "He must work out." Then he patted the briefcase under his arm. "Why don't we get down to business and deliver this to Mary. Maybe she'll invite us in for some tea and strumpets."

"Okay," Harry said. "Where does she live?"

Lloyd frowned uncertainly.

"Well, what's her last name?" Harry asked. "We'll look her up in the phone book."

"Hmmm." Lloyd thought hard. "You know, I don't really—I think it started with an S. Swan—Swans—" He peered at the label on the briefcase. "Oh, it's right here. *Samsonite*. Boy, I was way off. But I knew it started with an S."

Harry flipped through a phone book. "I don't see it here."

"She must be unlisted," Lloyd said. "But, hey, this looks like a friendly town. People will be *happy* to help!"

They asked everyone they saw, but nobody seemed to know a Mary Samsonite. Finally, they found themselves on the banks of an icy river, huddled around a fire for warmth.

Lloyd opened a tiny ketchup packet and squirted it into a coffee cup. Then he added a few drops of water and mixed it up. "What'd I tell you, Har?" he said. "People here are nice."

"The guy at that restaurant just *gave* you all that ketchup?" Harry couldn't believe such generosity.

Lloyd nodded. "Yep. Said we could take all we wanted—as long as we didn't hang around." He finished stirring and handed the cup to Harry. "Well, soup's on!"

"Mmm-mmm, good." Harry tried to swallow some.

"Yes sirree." Lloyd smiled bravely. "Everything sure seems to taste better when you're hungry!"

"Come on, Lloyd, it's really not that good," Harry pointed out.

Lloyd slurped up the last bit of the soup.

"And you know what the worst part is?" Harry asked.

Lloyd stared off into the distance and burped.

"We don't even know when our next meal will be. I've had it—I'm hungry and freezing." Harry rubbed his hands together. "I can't move my fingers anymore, Lloyd. They're all green and numb."

"Maybe you should wear these extra gloves I have." Lloyd pulled off the top pair he wore. "My hands have been getting kind of sweaty."

"Extra gloves!" Harry shrieked. "I'll kill you!"

"Calm down, Harry," Lloyd said. "Please, don't get so excited. I'm trying to eat."

Frustrated, Harry grabbed the briefcase and headed for the river. "I'm going to get rid of this stupid thing," he said. "It's been the root of our problems all along."

"Harry, hold up!" Lloyd said and chased after him. "Things are going to get better, I promise!"

Harry tried to throw the briefcase off the bridge, but Lloyd tackled him. The briefcase went flying. Harry and Lloyd wrestled, rolling over and over in the snow.

"I used to have a life," Harry complained, his hands around Lloyd's throat. "A miserable one, but a *life*, nonetheless!"

Then Lloyd's eyes lit up. "Harry, look!"

Harry glanced over at the briefcase, which was lying open on the snow, revealing stacks and stacks of hundred-dollar bills!

"Wow." Harry and Lloyd both made a dive for the cash.

When they had gathered up the money, they hurried back into town, clutching the briefcase. The city was lit with millions of tiny lights, like a fantasy winter wonderland.

"Here's the plan," Lloyd said. "We'll borrow a few bucks—just a small loan—from the briefcase and check into a cheap motel. And we'll keep track of the money we spend with IOUs."

Harry agreed. "We'll be meticulous—right down to the last penny."

"Whatever we borrow, we can pay back," Lloyd

vowed. "Isn't that so, Harry?"

"Absolutely," said Harry. "We're good for it."

"You know, as soon as we get jobs," Lloyd finished. They both shook hands.

A few minutes later, they had checked into the most expensive hotel in Aspen. A tuxedoed bell captain, Barnard, led them to an enormous and lavish suite.

"This is the Hotel Danbury's presidential suite, gentlemen," Barnard announced. "It's normally reserved for royalty, visiting dignitaries, and illustrious stars of stage and—"

"We'll take it," Lloyd snapped.

Barnard nodded. "Very good, sir. Are there any bags you'd like sent up?"

"No thanks, Barnard," Lloyd replied. "But I'll tell you what you can send up, my friend. How about some chow? Just bring us one of everything."

Harry glared at him. "One *of everything?*"

"Oh, sorry," Lloyd said and paused. "Make that *two* of everything."

Harry grinned, pleased with himself, and Lloyd stuffed a hundred-dollar bill into Barnard's jacket pocket.

"There you go," he said. "There's a little something for yourself, Barney."

"Yes, sir!" Barnard answered energetically. "Thank you, sir!" Then he bowed and scurried out of the room.

Harry opened the briefcase and inserted a small piece of paper. "Our first IOU," he said proudly. "Signed and dated!"

"*This* is the life," Lloyd declared with a huge smile on his face.

"And it was so simple," Harry added. "All it took was someone else's money!"

CHAPTER NINE

The next day Lloyd and Harry decided to *really enjoy* their new lifestyle. They spent all day shopping. They returned to the hotel in a brand-new Lamborghini. They got out, wearing their newly purchased, trendy ski garb in splashy fluorescent colors. They also wore fur boots and the latest NASA-designed goggles.

Several hotel employees rushed out to help them carry the shopping bags to the presidential suite. Then they lined up and Lloyd tipped them handsomely. Meanwhile, Harry filled out some more IOUs, tucking them inside the briefcase.

"It's really true," Harry said. "Last night I thought I was dreaming."

Lloyd grinned at him. "We've finally cracked the big time."

Harry lit a cigar with a 20-dollar bill and took a hearty puff. "You know," he said, blowing the bill out and tossing it off the balcony, "I think you might've gone a little overboard with the spending today." Harry inhaled his cigar again.

"What's the big deal?" Lloyd asked. "We're going to pay it all back, right?"

"True." Harry started coughing up smoke. "What am I thinking?"

There was a knock on the door.

"Enter, *parlez-vous!*" Lloyd called loudly.

Barnard came in with a champagne bucket and a newspaper.

"*Thank you,*" Lloyd said and gave him a hundred-dollar tip.

"I brought you your newspaper and some champagne, gentlemen," Barnard said. "Unfortunately, we didn't seem to have the, um, label you requested."

Lloyd frowned. "All out of Boone's Farm, hunh?" He had named one of the cheapest wines you could buy.

"You have a sharp wit, sir," Barnard said with a smile. "I took the liberty of bringing a substitute: Dom Perignon." It was the world's most expensive champagne. He put the tray down and handed Lloyd the newspaper.

"You can dispense with the 'sir' stuff," Harry said. "We're all from the same mold, Barney." He winked. "We just have a little more dough than you do right now."

Barnard bowed and left the room.

"Well, Har, this is the night," Lloyd said, popping open the champagne. "We're going to seize the day, take this town by the tail, and swing it around till it begs for mercy or snaps off and slams into a wall. We're going to go out there and make history, pal. This is going to be the greatest night of our lives!"

Harry looked up from the newspaper. "Hey, Lloyd, it says there's a two-part *Blossom* on tonight."

"Oh." Lloyd thought about that. "Okay. We'll stay in. But *tomorrow* we'll seize the day!"

After *Blossom*, an AT&T commercial came on. It was a real tearjerker about a kid calling his mother from college. Harry and Lloyd bawled their eyes out, deeply moved. But once the commercial ended, they stopped crying instantly.

"So," Harry said. "What's on next?"

"I don't know." Lloyd picked up the newspaper. "Let me have a look." He started reading, and then suddenly his jaw dropped. "Harry, it's her! Look!"

Harry leaned over and read the headline: SWANSONS TO HOST PRESERVATIONISTS' GALA TOMORROW NIGHT; CITY'S ELITE EXPECTED. Below the article there was a photograph of Mary. She was with her parents, and the three of them were posing with two beautiful, snowy white owls.

"Mary *Swanson*," Lloyd said, remembering her name now.

"Come on, Cinderella." Harry turned the television off. "It's time to get *you* ready for the ball!"

They spent the entire next day getting ready for the gala event. First the hotel barbers came up to their room and gave them fresh bowl haircuts. When the attendants lifted the dryers from their heads, the guys had elaborate new hairdos. Lloyd mussed up Harry's hair, and Harry did the same to Lloyd's. By the end of the fight their hair looked exactly the way it always had.

Lloyd was being shaved by an attendant with a straight razor. Suddenly he grabbed his neck as if he'd been nicked. Blood squirted out between his fingers, and the attendant gasped in horror. Lloyd laughed—there was a squeeze bottle of ketchup hidden in his hand. Harry found this prank equally hilarious, but the attendant was not amused.

After goofing around with their beauticians, Lloyd and Harry were dressed to impress, ready to party.

Harry wore a sky-blue tuxedo, while Lloyd had decided on pumpkin-orange. They also had matching top hats and canes.

Lloyd and Harry headed over to the gala. Hundreds of guests in black tie and elegant gowns filed into the Aspen Preservation Society mansion. Lloyd and Harry pulled up in their Lamborghini. Their fancy car stopped, Barnard at the wheel. They handed him a couple of hundred dollars.

"Thanks for the lift, Barney!" Lloyd said cheerfully.

Nicholas Andre was greeting people at the door. He stopped Lloyd and Harry before they went inside.

"Excuse me, gentlemen," he said, giving them the once-over, "but this is a five-hundred-dollar-a-plate dinner."

Harry and Lloyd looked at each other and shrugged. Lloyd took out a wad of bills and peeled off 20 hundreds.

"Put us down for four plates," he said. "In case we want seconds." Before going inside, he took out his breath spray and squirted it toward his mouth. He missed, and the spray hit Andre in the eyes. Naturally, Lloyd didn't notice.

But Andre's associate, J. P. Shay, had noticed. She ran up beside him, an alarmed expression on her face. "It's them, boss," she gasped.

Andre pulled out a silk handkerchief and wiped the breath spray from his face. "Just keep an eye on them," he snapped.

Inside, Harry and Lloyd were impressed by the crowd.

"This is our big chance," Lloyd said. "All we gotta do is show a little class and sophistication."

"No problem, Lloyd." Harry belched.

They turned at the sound of a clinking glass at the front of the room. Andre stood at a podium. There was a large, covered box next to him on side. Mr. and Mrs. Swanson were standing on his other side.

"If I could have your attention, please," Andre said into the microphone, raising his hands for quiet. "I'd like to thank you all for coming to this very special event. As you know, the Aspen Preservation Society—founded and funded by our great benefactors Karl and Helen Swanson—is the world's foremost defender of 23 endangered species. Tonight we are deeply honored to welcome our 24th."

The crowd applauded as Mr. Swanson took Andre's place.

"Ladies and gentlemen, I give you the Icelandic snow owl!" Andre pulled the cover from the large box, revealing two majestic, fluffy white owls in a huge cage. "These magnificent specimens were rescued recently, after a five-year, two-million-dollar effort on our part. Together they constitute one-seventh of the snow-owl population left on the planet. We hope we will soon see these wonderful creatures flourish once more!"

There was loud applause.

"Again, thank you, and enjoy your evening," Mr. Swanson said. "Oh, and feel free to take a closer look at our new friends here. Enjoy!"

The crowd began to mingle again. Instead of meeting and greeting, Harry and Lloyd headed straight for the bar.

"A bowl of trail mix, please," Lloyd ordered. He looked at Harry. "Have you ever wondered why you and I never have long-term girlfriends?"

"Hey, I went out with Fraida Felcher for two and a half *weeks*," Harry protested.

"That was a fluke," Lloyd said. "The reason is that we're afraid of the C word. *Commitment*."

Harry completely agreed—and was completely happy about it.

"Well, *I'm* ready for commitment, Harry," Lloyd argued. "The first time I laid eyes on Mary Swanson, I got that old-fashioned romantic feeling, where I just knew she was going to be my main squeeze."

Harry looked impressed. "Wow. That's a special feeling, Lloyd."

"Yup," Lloyd said, crunching some trail mix. He suddenly stopped in mid-chew as he spotted someone across the room—someone special.

It was Mary Swanson, looking more beautiful than ever, wearing a spectacular black dress.

"Oh, my," he whispered. "There she is!"

CHAPTER TEN

Harry gasped. He whirled around to check out Mary Swanson for himself.

"Wow, you weren't kidding. She's an angel!" He grinned and nudged Lloyd. "Well, what are you waiting for? Get over there and talk to her."

Lloyd hung back. "She'll think I'm some kind of psycho when she realizes how far I came just to see her."

"You have her briefcase," Harry reminded him. "She's going to be *thrilled*."

"Hey, I have an idea," Lloyd said. "You go over and introduce yourself. You can build me up, so later I won't have to brag. Tell her I'm good-looking, and I'm rich."

Harry agreed. Straightening his polka-dot bow tie, he headed over to where Mary was standing, by the owls' cage.

"Hey, there, good-lookin', what's cookin'?" he asked.

Mary's eyebrows went up. "I beg your pardon?"

"Pretty owls," Harry said, indicating the cage.

"Yeah." Mary smiled politely. "Are you a bird lover?"

"Well, I used to have a parakeet, but my main area of expertise is canines," Harry told her. "That's *dogs*, to the layperson."

"Canines," Mary repeated, pretending she'd never heard the word before. "I'll have to remember that."

"Yeah, it's important," Harry agreed. "Anyway, the real reason I came over is that I want to introduce you to a buddy of mine."

At that moment Mary's stepmother, Helen, appeared.

"I don't believe I've met your friend, Mary," she said.

"Actually, we haven't been introduced yet." Mary held out her hand. "I'm Mary Swanson, and this is my stepmother, Helen."

Harry shook hands with them. "Harry Dunne. Pleasure meeting you both."

"I saw you come in earlier, Mr. Dunne," Helen remarked. "I was hoping we'd get a chance to talk."

Harry looked confused. "You were?"

"That tuxedo," Helen explained. "I love a man with a sense of humor."

Mary shot Helen a warning look before smiling sweetly at Harry. For a moment he was caught up in her blue eyes. Then he snapped out of it.

"About my friend," he started to say.

Helen promptly interrupted him. "Are you doing anything tomorrow, Mr. Dunne? Because I believe Mary's looking for somebody to hit the slopes with."

Mary blushed. "Helen, you're embarrassing me."

"Well, you are, aren't you?" Helen said. "I mean, after all, the snow will be gone in a week or two, and this is probably your last chance." She turned to Harry. "So, what do you say, Harry? Are you available?"

"Uh, I don't know," he answered. "You see, my friend—"

"Forget your friends for one day," Helen said briskly. "You and Mary will have a ball—"

Mary's eyes met his, waiting for an answer.

"Um, well—I—I don't know," Harry stammered. "You see, the thing is, I—sure. Why not?"

With that decided, he said good night to the two of them and went back to the bar, where Lloyd waited impatiently.

"How come you didn't bring her over?" Lloyd wanted to know.

"Relax, you're golden," Harry told him. "I got you a date with her tomorrow."

For a few seconds Lloyd was speechless. "That's—I mean—it's—" He broke into a huge grin. "I love you, Har!" He clasped Harry in a tight embrace. "I love you!"

"Okay, okay," Harry muttered. "Get a grip, Lloyd. You're making a scene."

Lloyd stepped back, elated. "You're going to be my best man, Har, I promise," he cried. "You just earned a seat at the head table. And we've already got our tuxedos. This calls for a bit of the bubbly!"

He grabbed a bottle of champagne from a nearby bucket and struggled to open it. The cork shot out of the bottle and zipped across the room like a bullet—right at one of the priceless Icelandic snow owls. There was a strangled *squawk!* and then a heavy *thump!*

A hush fell over the entire party. Everyone turned to the cage, too stunned to speak. Feathers floated in the air, and one of the magnificent owls lay on its back, motionless. The species was now one bird closer to extinction.

Oblivious of what they had done, Harry and Lloyd clinked their champagne glasses together.

Harry yawned. "Well, I think I'm going to turn in."

"Yeah, me too," Lloyd agreed. "Big day tomorrow."

They headed for the door.

"Boy, this party really died," Lloyd remarked.

The rest of the room still hadn't figured out what had happened—except for Nicholas Andre, who had been watching Lloyd and Harry's every move. He looked *extremely* unhappy.

J. P. Shay moved over to join him. "Maybe it was just a coincidence?"

Andre shook his head. "Don't be stupid. It's a message, plain and simple—Mental killed their bird, now they killed ours."

"But how could anybody kill a bird with a cork?" Shay asked.

Andre ran his fingers through his hair, looking like he was at his wit's end. "These guys aren't just anybody. They're good. Look at what they did to Mental—and he was the best."

"But they already have our money," Shay pointed out. "What more could they want?"

"I don't know." Andre felt a shiver of fear as he watched them leave. "But we'd better find out!"

The next morning Lloyd stood in front of the mirror in the presidential suite, primping for his date.

"Mary Christmas," he said aloud, testing out his last name with hers. "Mrs. Mary Christmas. It's kind of catchy, don't you think, Har?"

"It's nice," Harry replied, busily putting on his new ski clothes. "But maybe you're jumping the gun a little. I mean, who knows, once you get to know her, you may find out she's not your type."

Lloyd thrust an angry finger at him. "Don't you ever say that again. She is the love of my life, the blood in my veins. We belong together, till the mountains fall into the sea, till the heavens collide, till I get sick of her and need to move on."

He paused. "Now let me get this straight. The Avalanche Bar and Grill downstairs?"

Harry nodded. "Ten o'clock sharp."

Lloyd noticed Harry's outfit. "Where are you going dressed like that?"

Harry looked self-conscious. "I, uh, thought I'd try my luck on the slopes."

Lloyd stared at him. "You mean you're going out in public dressed in *tights?*"

"They're fashionable Euro-trash ski trousers," Harry said huffily.

"Right." Lloyd checked his reflection one last time. "Well, later, Har. Thanks for *everything*. I owe you, buddy."

Harry felt a stab of guilt. "Don't mention it," he muttered.

Once he was sure Lloyd was gone, Harry hurried down to the parking lot. Mary was going to be at the Aspen base lodge, waiting for him, and he didn't want to be late!

◀CHAPTER ELEVEN▶

Inside the base lodge, people were milling about, getting ready for a day on the slopes. Dozens of pairs of skis were lined up against the wall behind them. Mary sat near the fireplace, wearing a gorgeous new ski outfit.

Harry, already wearing his skis, made his way through the room toward her. His progress was one long series of stumbles, crashes, and hasty apologies. When he finally reached Mary's side, he was out of breath.

"Sorry I'm late." He pointed at his skis. "It's really hard driving a clutch with these things on."

"Uh, right," she said. "Well, come on."

Together they made their way outside to the slopes. When it was their turn to get on the chair lift, Harry crouched down beside Mary nervously. The chair came up behind them and made a smooth pickup—of Mary. Harry, blushing furiously, was left alone, still in the crouching position. He had missed the ride. To cover up his embarrassment, he quickly pretended to be stretching his muscles.

"You take the first run alone," he called after her. "I'm going to loosen up first."

At ten o'clock, Lloyd nervously entered the Avalanche Bar and Grill. He looked around. The place was completely empty, so he took a seat at the bar.

Maybe his beloved Mary was just running late.

Out on the slopes, Harry and Mary stood in line again. This time, Harry managed to get onto the chair lift—although he almost fell off.

"It feels so good to be up here." Mary took a deep breath of mountain air. "I haven't been out-doors much lately."

"Why not?" Harry asked.

"There've been...family problems," Mary said evasively. "I don't want to bore you with them."

Harry understood. "Thanks," he told her. Looking down, he noticed a patch of frost on the chair-lift bar. "Oh, look. Frost!" He licked it, and his tongue immediately fused with the frozen metal.

"Are you okay?" Mary asked.

"Thure," Harry lisped, trying to tug his tongue free. "I do thith all the time."

When they got to the top of the hill, Mary dis-embarked, but Harry, his tongue still stuck, was forced to stay on.

"Are you sure you're going to be okay?" she asked.

"Oh, yeth," Harry lisped. "I'll rathe you to the bottom." Then he and the chair lift swung around and started heading down the hill again.

So far his date had not been very much fun.

Lloyd waited in the bar for hours, but Mary never showed up. He was about to give up and leave, when a beautiful woman slid onto the stool next to his. It was the athletic beauty Harry had tried to pick up at the truck stop.

"Hi there," she said.

Lloyd just grunted, too upset to answer.

"Bad day, hunh?" she said sympathetically. "Me too. Of course, every day's a bad day for me since I split up with my boyfriend." She paused. "Are you a good listener?"

Lloyd groaned and covered his head with his arms.

At about that same time, Mary was gracefully carving her way to the bottom of the ski trail. She stopped in a spray of snow and searched the mountainside for Harry.

He was sitting at an outdoor table, his tongue still attached to the chair lift, which had been removed from the cable by the ski patrol. He was trying to drink a cup of coffee—and trying to act as if everything were normal. His eyes were pinned on a mime who was performing for the lunchtime crowd.

"Harry, are you okay?" Mary asked.

"Oh, I'm fine, I'm fine," he said, and patted the chair-lift seat beside him. "Thaved a theat for you."

What Harry couldn't see was that high up on the hill J. P. Shay was aiming a high-powered rifle at him.

"Your luck just ran out, pal," Shay said softly.

In the meantime, Mary was trying to get Harry loose.

"Relax," Mary said. "It'll hurt for just a moment." Grabbing his head in both hands, she started pulling it away from the bar. Harry moaned in pain.

His tongue stretched, and stretched, and then suddenly yanked free. He and Mary fell backward—out of the path of Shay's bullet as it whizzed by. The bullet hit the mime, who shrieked at the top of his lungs.

"Better?" Mary asked.

"Yeth." Harry rubbed his sore mouth. "Much."

Feeling better, Harry took Mary for a stroll. Mary playfully tossed a tiny snowball at Harry, and he fired a huge iceball back at her head. Angrily, she whipped one back, and he mashed her face into a pile of snow, stuffing handfuls down her back.

Finally, he was starting to enjoy himself!

In the Avalanche Bar and Grill, Lloyd had put his head on the bar. Next to him, the beautiful woman rambled on, and on, and on.

"Anyway," she continued, "after my boyfriend backed into my garage for the third time, you know what I said to myself?"

Lloyd groaned. "No, and I don't care."

"Well, he comes home that night," she went on, "and he decides he wants to fix the sink. So *I* said—"

Lloyd motioned to the bartender. "Hey! You wouldn't happen to know a Mary Swanson, would you?"

"Sure," the bartender said. "They've got that big place up on Alpine Drive."

"Thanks." Lloyd threw down a 100-dollar bill on his way out.

The sun was setting as Harry dropped Mary off at her family's mountainside chalet. She beamed at him and kissed his cheek.

"So, you'll pick me up tonight at seven forty-five?" she asked.

"I've got a few things to take care of first," he said. "Better make it quarter to eight." He watched, lovestruck, as she walked into the house. "Mary Dunne," he mused. "Mrs. Mary Dunne. Got a nice ring to it."

Hiding in some nearby bushes, Lloyd watched in shocked disbelief. He had been betrayed by his very best friend in the world!

◄ CHAPTER TWELVE ►

When Harry got back to the presidential suite, he found Lloyd looking sad and forlorn. Lloyd explained how he had been stood up.

"Are you sure you went to the right bar?" Harry asked.

"I'm pretty sure." Lloyd sighed deeply. "Maybe she just had second thoughts."

Harry paced back and forth as though deeply puzzled. "Wait a minute," he said. "She must've meant ten o'clock at *night*." He shook his head, trying to sound convincing. "Boy, aren't *we* a couple of beauties, hunh?"

"And all this time I've been going through so much pain and personal anguish." Lloyd pretended to be relieved. "Ha! It was all just a simple misunderstanding."

Harry nodded wisely. "That'll teach you to jump to conclusions."

Harry walked into the closet to change his clothes, and Lloyd clenched his fist and glared after him. Lloyd was fuming. His best friend was now his worst enemy.

"Since you're busy tonight, think I'll go catch a flick," Harry called from inside the closet.

Lloyd scowled and went over to the bar, where he filled two mugs with coffee—and something else. The kind of medicine that made you go to the bathroom—a lot.

"Hey, old buddy, old pal," he said, dumping an entire package of the medicine into one of the mugs. "Care to join me in a good-luck toast before you head out?"

Harry came out of the closet dressed in a flashy new suit and tie. "Sure thing, pal of mine, friend forever."

Lloyd handed him the mug with the medicine. "To my friend, Harry, the matchmaker," he toasted, lifting his own mug.

Harry felt a pang of guilt but drank up anyway. "Tastes great," he lied, setting the empty mug down.

"Less filling," Lloyd responded automatically.

On his way over to pick up Mary, Harry felt a little sick to his stomach, but decided that it was just nerves.

Mary opened the front door with a big smile. "Make yourself at home," she said. "I'll be ready in a minute."

Harry nodded and followed her inside. But then he felt so ill that he rushed into the nearest bathroom. Something had *definitely* disagreed with him.

"Are you in there, Harry?" Mary called through the door.

"Be right out!" he answered.

Just then the doorbell rang, and Mary went to answer it.

Lloyd stood on the front steps, looking dapper in his fashionable new clothes.

"Hi," he said. "Remember me?"

Mary looked confused. "Not really."

"Providence," he reminded her. "I drove you to the airport."

"Oh," Mary brightened. "Lloyd, right? What are you doing in Aspen?"

Lloyd smiled proudly. "I brought you your briefcase. You left it at the airport, so I picked it up for you."

Mary's mouth dropped open. "You're the one who took it?"

"Yeah, it's back at my hotel room," Lloyd said. "Why don't you jump on the bike with me and we'll go get it."

Mary was torn. Should she get her briefcase or wait for Harry? Then she made up her mind and hurried down to the bathroom. "Sorry, Harry," she said through the door. "Something important's come up and I have to run out. It's sort of an emergency. I promise we'll do this another time, okay? Sorry."

With that, she was gone.

Harry, who was washing his hands, slumped against the sink, defeated. "Great," he muttered sadly. "Just great."

When Lloyd and Mary reached the Hotel Danbury, neither of them noticed that they were being followed by Nicholas Andre and J. P. Shay.

Andre smiled and pulled a pistol from beneath his coat. "They're mine," he told Shay, falling into step behind them.

Lloyd led Mary upstairs to the suite and right to the closed briefcase, which lay on the bed.

"So, anyway," he said, "I tried to look you up when I got here, but I didn't know your last name."

Mary beamed at him, unable to believe that she actually had the briefcase back. "This is incredible," she said. "You mean to say you drove 2,000 miles just for me?"

Lloyd shrugged modestly. "Well—I didn't really have anything else to do. And I know how frustrating it can be to lose a bag."

Mary leaned over and kissed him on the cheek. "That is so sweet, Lloyd. Really."

Lloyd was so overcome that he couldn't help telling her the whole story, although he didn't have enough nerve to look her in the eye while he was doing it. "Look, Mary, I know this may seem a little sudden," he said, turning his back, "but I've given it a lot of thought. You're the woman

I've been waiting for my whole life, and I'm not ashamed to admit it. I'm *crazy* about you. I've never felt this way about anyone." He laughed nervously and ducked his head. "Listen to me, I feel like a schoolboy again."

Just then Mary came out of the kitchenette carrying a glass of water. She was surprised to find Lloyd alone in the room.

"I thought I heard you talking to someone," she said.

Lloyd swallowed, realizing he had to start over. "Mary, I—I really *like* you," he blurted out. "I'm going to ask you something flat out, and I want you to answer me honestly. What do you think the chances are of a girl like you and a guy like me ending up together?"

Mary blinked. She was obviously thrown by the question.

"Come on, give it to me straight," Lloyd said. "What are my chances?"

"Not good," she answered.

Lloyd frowned. "You mean like one out of a hundred?"

"More like one out of a million," Mary said honestly.

Lloyd frowned harder. "So you're telling me there *is* a chance?" He smiled slyly.

There was a knock at the door, and when Lloyd opened it, he was face-to-face with Nicholas Andre.

A look of surprise swept over Mary's face. "Nicholas, what are you doing here?"

"I've been looking for you, Mary," he said. "I've got some very interesting news about your husband."

"Husband?" Lloyd repeated, devastated by the news. "You have a husband?"

Andre took out his pistol and pointed it at them. "Aren't you two going to invite me in?" he asked with a nasty smile.

Downstairs, Harry slouched his way into the hotel lobby. *I probably deserved that dose of medicine*, he told himself. After all, he had turned against his best friend. But he still felt lousy about missing out on his date. He also still felt sick.

"Hey!" a woman shouted across the room.

Harry turned to see the beautiful woman from the truck stop and the bar approaching him. "You...?" he asked, startled. "What are you doing here?"

In the presidential suite Andre kept his gun pointed at a stunned Lloyd and Mary.

"Who are you?" Lloyd asked bravely. "What do you want?"

"Don't play dumb with me," Andre snapped. "I'm the rightful owner of that briefcase you've been carrying!"

Mary just stared. She couldn't believe what was happening.

"Nicholas!" she cried out. "My family trusted you!"

"Uh, listen, Mr. Samsonite," Lloyd said, "I just want you to know that my friend Harry and I have *every* intention of reimbursing you."

"Open it!" Andre ordered Mary. "Now!"

Mary opened the briefcase with a trembling hand. Out fell a pile of crumpled-up balls of white paper, along with only a few packets of hundreds.

"Where's all the money?" Andre asked furiously. He kicked the briefcase.

"That's as good as money, sir," Lloyd assured him. "Those are our IOUs. Why, every penny's accounted for."

Andre's eyes widened in anger. His cheeks flushed red. He took aim and cocked the hammer on the gun, getting ready to fire.

"You're dead, man!" he yelled.

CHAPTER THIRTEEN

Harry burst into the hotel room like a man who really needed to talk. There was a contrite expression on his face.

"Lloyd, are you home?" he called. "We've gotta talk, man. I have a serious confession to make." He stopped. Lloyd and Mary were sitting on the bed, their arms handcuffed to the bedpost. "Oh, good. You found her!"

Andre stepped out from behind him and shoved the muzzle of the gun into Harry's back. "Why don't you stay and join our little party," he suggested. "You're *just* in time for the killing part."

Harry raised his hands in surrender. He collapsed onto the bed, unable to look Lloyd in the eye.

Andre picked up the telephone and ordered his getaway ticket—one-way to Amsterdam. He kept his gun trained on them the entire time.

"Wait. You mean you two know each other?" Mary asked.

"Yeah," Lloyd said stiffly. "We used to be best friends."

Harry nodded. "Until he turned into a back stabber."

Lloyd stared at him. "*Me*, a back stabber? I saw her first."

"Hey, I can't help it if she found me irresistible," Harry said, shrugging.

Mary just rolled her eyes.

"Besides," Harry went on, "you knew how crazy I was about Fraida Felcher, and that didn't stop *you*, did it?"

Lloyd flushed. "Look, I was going to tell you about that. It was going to be mentioned at the reading of my will. I swear—you can ask my lawyer."

"Well," Harry said sadly, "I guess we both learned a little something about each other, didn't we?"

"You said it, pal," Lloyd agreed. "Maybe we're not as good friends as we thought we were. I mean, if one beautiful girl could rip us apart like this, our friendship isn't worth much." He shook his head. "Maybe we should call it quits right here."

"Just tell me where to sign, bud," Harry said grimly.

Andre hung up the phone and re-cocked his gun. "Okay," he said, "which one of you losers wants to die first?"

"If you kill us, you'd be killing yourself," Harry said.

Andre looked confused—and so did Mary and Lloyd.

"You see," Harry explained, "philosophers believe that we're all really just tiny pieces of one huge universal being. In other words, I am you and you are me, so if you were to kill us, you'd be committing suicide."

"Thanks," Andre said impatiently. "Now I know who to kill first."

"What about my husband?" Mary asked. "Did you kill him too?"

Harry sat up straighter. "Husband? What husband?" Then he scowled. "In that case, why don't you kill her first?"

"No, I'll go first, Harry," Lloyd said. "I'm the one who got you into this mess."

Andre pointed the gun at Lloyd.

"No, wait, do me first," Harry said. "I'm the one who stole your girl, Lloyd. I *deserve* it."

Andre sighed and pointed the gun at Harry. As Lloyd and Mary looked on in horror, he fired twice. Harry grabbed his stomach and fell onto the floor.

"You monster!" Lloyd screamed. "You killed my best friend!"

Andre smiled at him. "If it's any consolation, you're about to be reunited." He aimed the gun at Lloyd, his finger twitching on the trigger.

Suddenly Harry popped up and fired six quick shots—all of which missed.

"Harry, you're alive!" Lloyd cried. "You have a gun!" He paused. "And you're a terrible shot."

"Lucky for *me*," Andre said, looking at the damage around him.

The door burst open, and police officers stormed in with their weapons drawn, shouting for everyone to get their hands up. Behind them came the beautiful woman. She pushed her way through the mass of cops, flashing an ID badge.

"Special Agent Beth Jordan!" she said crisply. "F.B.I.! Good work, Harry."

Harry opened his shirt, revealing a bulletproof vest. "She grabbed me down in the lobby and explained what was up," he told Lloyd and Mary. "They put this on me and gave me a gun."

Lloyd stared at Agent Jordan. "But how did you...?"

"We've been following you two all the way from Providence," she said. "Mr. and Mrs. Swanson had a homing device planted in the briefcase."

Harry and Lloyd gave each other guilty looks.

"About that dough," Harry started to say.

"Every single bill was counterfeit," Agent Jordan said.

"That's great!" Lloyd exclaimed. "We'll get some jobs, buy a printing press, and, well, make it up in no time!"

Agent Jordan groaned, shaking her head.

A crowd gathered in the lobby as Andre and J. P. Shay were taken away in handcuffs. While Mary talked to the police, Harry and Lloyd stared at her lovingly.

"You were right, Lloyd," Harry said. "She was definitely worth the trip."

"She's something," Lloyd agreed. "I'm glad we could help her out."

Another police cruiser pulled up, and a huge, muscle-bound man climbed out of the back seat. He was massaging the back of his aching neck and brushing Styrofoam peanuts out of his hair.

Mary ran over to greet him. "Bobby! You're okay!"

"Yeah, baby, I'm fine." He readjusted his neck with a gruesome crack. "Just a little sore, that's all."

Mary looked around for Lloyd. "Honey," she said to Bobby, "there's someone I want to introduce you to. He's one of the sweetest, gentlest men I've ever known."

Lloyd stared into space. He had lost Mary.

"Lloyd," Mary spoke more loudly. "I said, this is my husband."

Lloyd forced a weak smile. "Hi, Bobby," he said. "I'm—so happy for you."

As endings went, it wasn't the one he would have chosen.

* * *

100

The next day, when Lloyd and Harry stepped out of the hotel elevator with their meager luggage, nobody rushed to their aid. They crept through the lobby, trying to sneak past Barnard.

"Hello, gentlemen." Barnard stepped in front of them before they could escape to the parking lot.

Lloyd and Harry stopped, looking sheepish.

"Listen, we really appreciate all you did for us during our stay," Lloyd said.

Harry nodded. "And we're, um, sorry the money we gave you turned out to be phony."

"Don't worry about it," Barnard assured them. "The Swanson family has promised to reimburse everyone."

Lloyd and Harry grinned in surprise.

"Great," Lloyd said.

"Superb," Harry agreed.

"What are you two going to do now?" Barnard asked.

The boys looked at each other.

"I don't know," Harry admitted. "We have no talents, and we don't really fit in socially."

"Maybe we'll be film critics," Lloyd said.

"Maybe you should stay right here," Barnard suggested.

Harry and Lloyd exchanged glances again.

"Uh—this joint is a little out of our budget, Barney," Lloyd said wryly.

"I think we might be able to find you a free room somewhere. After all"—Barnard winked at them—"we're all from the same mold. You just don't have any dough right now."

"Are you on the level?" Harry asked, stunned by the generous offer.

"Absolutely," Barnard beamed. "Provided, of course, you don't mind working one afternoon a week."

Harry and Lloyd stopped smiling.

"Doing what?" Harry asked uneasily.

"Well...doing what I do," Barnard said. "I'll train you myself."

Harry and Lloyd locked eyes.

"Uh, isn't there anything else?" Harry asked.

Lloyd nodded. "Yeah. Something with more dignity?"

Barnard shook his head, losing all patience with them.

"Maybe you guys should just try your luck down the road...."

Harry and Lloyd agreed. They headed for their minibike. It was clearly time to move on. Lloyd started the engine and they both climbed aboard.

"Now that we're finished elbow-rubbing," Harry said as they started down the road, "what's next, Lloyd?"

Lloyd shrugged. "I say we go to Mexico and check out the northern lights."

"Good plan." Harry swerved the bike, and they chugged off into the sunset, heading toward their next adventure.